Squashed, Flat, Splat!

Written by Nick Crombie
Illustrated by Terry Burton

BRIMAX

Hippopotamus Meets the Elephant

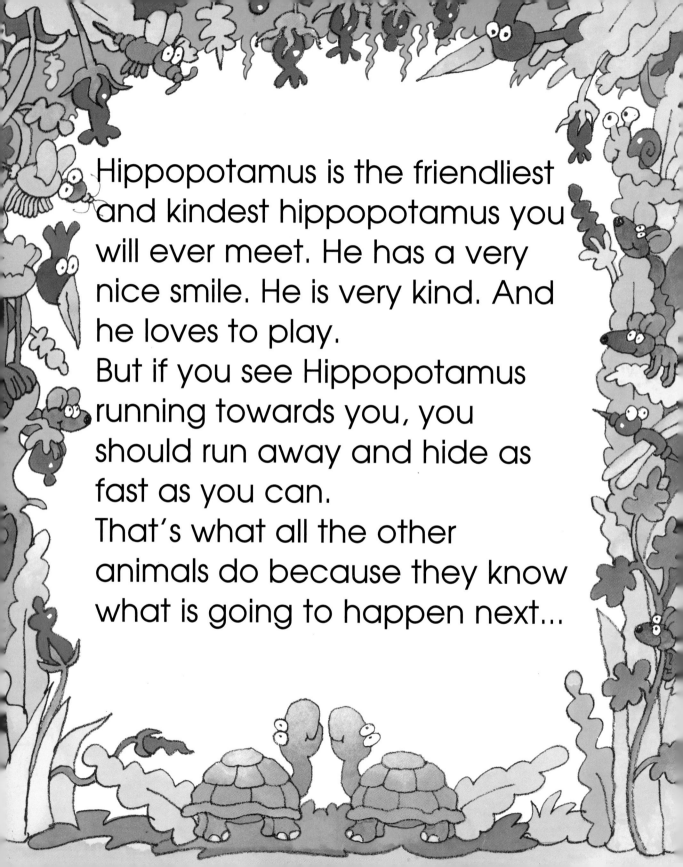

Hippopotamus is the friendliest and kindest hippopotamus you will ever meet. He has a very nice smile. He is very kind. And he loves to play.

But if you see Hippopotamus running towards you, you should run away and hide as fast as you can.

That's what all the other animals do because they know what is going to happen next...

First there is a rumbling noise,
and it grows louder and louder
- rumble, rumble, **rumble**.

Then there is a cloud of dust and it gets bigger, and bigger, and **bigger**.

And inside the cloud of dust is Hippopotamus. He is running faster, and faster, and **faster**, because he is so pleased to see you. And he is getting closer, and closer, and **closer.**
And he has a great big smile upon his face.

Then if you haven't run away,
he will jump in the air and land
right on top of you - and give
you a great big hug.
But what will happen to you?
You will be squashed as flat
as a piece of paper in this
book, because Hippopotamus
is so much bigger than you.
And he is very, very **heavy**.

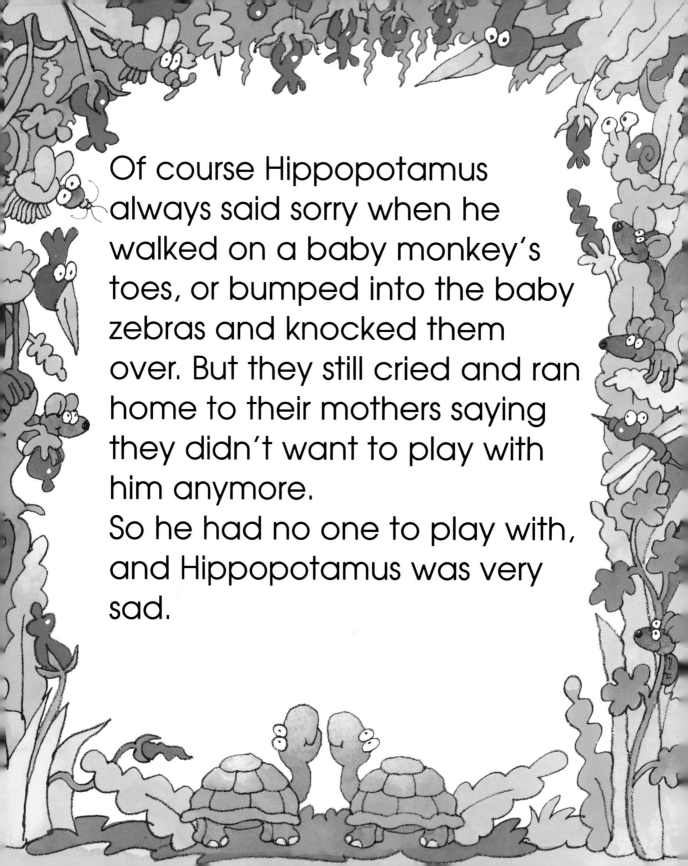

Of course Hippopotamus always said sorry when he walked on a baby monkey's toes, or bumped into the baby zebras and knocked them over. But they still cried and ran home to their mothers saying they didn't want to play with him anymore.

So he had no one to play with, and Hippopotamus was very sad.

Every day Hippopotamus sat by himself at the bottom of a tree with great, big tears rolling down his round cheeks. He didn't know how much it hurt to be squashed because nobody had ever squashed him - until one day he met Elephant.

On this particular day it was very hot and dry.
Hippopotamus was sitting under the tree as usual and since he was very thirsty he went to the pond to get a drink. There he saw Elephant having a swim.
Elephant didn't look very big because he was mostly under the water. Hippopotamus could only see his ears and trunk.
"Hello," said Hippopotamus. "Do you want to play a game with me?"

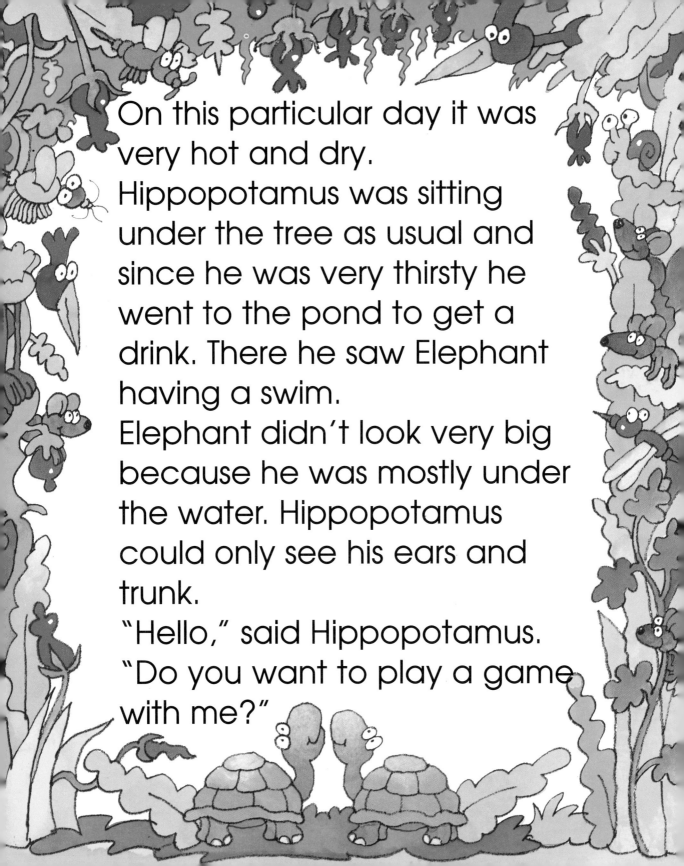

Elephant couldn't hear him because his ears were full of water.

Hippopotamus spoke louder. "HELLO! DO YOU WANT TO PLAY WITH ME?"

This time Elephant heard him. "Hello," he said. And he swam to the side of the pond and began to climb out.

As Elephant came out of the water, Hippopotamus saw that he was very big.

First there were his head and trunk. Then his huge, round body. And lastly there were four enormous legs, each one the size of a tree trunk. Hippopotamus suddenly felt very small.

"What game do you want to play?" asked Elephant, looking down at Hippopotamus.

"Shall we play catch?" replied Hippopotamus. "I like playing catch."

"Yes," said Elephant.

At first the game was great fun. Hippopotamus and Elephant ran backwards and forwards and round and round as fast as they could. Hippopotamus was very happy that he had someone to play with at last.

But then something happened. Hippopotamus fell over when Elephant was running after him. But Elephant was running so fast he couldn't stop.

Crash! He fell onto Hippopotamus and squashed him flat.

"Ow, ow, ow, please get off, you're hurting me!" cried Hippopotamus.

Elephant rolled over and stood up.

"I'm very sorry," he said. "It was an accident. I didn't mean to hurt you."

Hippopotamus made sure that nothing was broken and then he stood up.

"There, there," said Elephant. "I hope you feel better soon."

Hippopotamus did feel better. But now he knew that being squashed wasn't very nice. He also knew why the other animals wouldn't play with him anymore.

The next day Hippopotamus went to find them.

"Please come out wherever you are," he called. "I'm very sorry that I squashed all of you. I promise not to do it again."

One by one, the animals came out from where they had been hiding.

"Do you really promise?" asked a baby zebra.

"Yes, do you really promise?" asked a baby monkey.

"Yes," said Hippopotamus. "I will never squash you again. Please will you play with me now?"

The animals thought for a moment and then decided that they would play with him. And Hippopotamus didn't squash any of them ever again.

Heavy Hippopotamus

Hippopotamus is smooth and round, with four short legs, one at each corner.

He has a round face, big, brown eyes and a huge smile.

He has a squiggly tail.

Hippopotamus is very bouncy, but don't let him bounce on you unless you want to be as flat as a pancake - because he is VERY, VERY HEAVY.

One morning, Hippopotamus was doing his exercises. He bounced up and down - BOING, BOING, BOING.
Then he jumped up and down - UP DOWN THUD, UP DOWN THUD, UP DOWN THUD.
Then he ran around in circles - BADOOM, BADOOM, BADOOM.
That made him dizzy, and he fell over.

None of the other animals liked it when Hippopotamus did his exercises because it made the ground shake.

In fact it made the ground shake **so much** that the birds fell off the trees, the giraffes' necks wobbled from side to side, the zebras' stripes got mixed up, and it gave the lions headaches!

After his exercises Hippopotamus liked to have a long bath.
None of the animals liked this either. There was only room for Hippopotamus in the pond. None of the other animals could get in at the same time without being squashed. And by the time Hippopotamus had cleaned and scrubbed all his smelly bits, the water was full of muddy bubbles.

"Being clean is very important," said Hippopotamus. "If I didn't wash I'd be all muddy and smelly. Nobody would like that."

The other animals agreed. But **they** were muddy and smelly because they couldn't get into the pond to wash. So one day the animals decided they would have to find a way to stop Hippopotamus having his bath.

Late that night Hippopotamus heard lots of banging and sawing. He didn't care what was happening because he was very tired. So he went to sleep and he snored very loudly.

A little way away from where Hippopotamus was sleeping, an elephant put down his hammer. He turned to the monkeys, birds, zebras and giraffes standing next to him. "I think everything is ready now," he said. "I don't think Hippopotamus will want his bath tomorrow."

Very early the next morning, Hippopotamus woke up. Right away he started his exercises. He bounced up and down - BOING, BOING, BOING. Then he jumped up and down - UP DOWN THUD, UP DOWN THUD, UP DOWN THUD. Then he ran around in circles - BADOOM, BADOOM, BADOOM. That made him dizzy and he fell over.

"That's better," he said. "Time for my bath now."

He trotted over to the pond and was just about to jump in when he saw something which made him stop.

Right in the middle of the pond were some enormous teeth in an enormous mouth poking up from under the water.
They were the kind of teeth which could bite a hippopotamus and eat him all up.
They looked like the teeth of a crocodile who was hiding under the water. A crocodile just waiting for a hippopotamus to eat for its breakfast.

"Help!" cried Hippopotamus. "Help! There's a crocodile in the pond and I'm too frightened to go in it!"

The elephant heard Hippopotamus and came down to look.

"You're right," said the elephant. "It looks like a very big crocodile to me. You'd better not have your bath today."

All the animals who had come along to see what the noise was about agreed.

"Oh well," said Hippopotamus. "I don't suppose it will matter if I don't have a bath today. Maybe I could have one tomorrow instead if the crocodile has gone away."

"That's a good idea," said the elephant. "Why don't you go for a walk? There are some nice, juicy leaves to eat just over the hill."

"Yes," said Hippopotamus. "That's a very good idea." And off he went.

The animals waited by the pond until they were sure he had gone. Then one by one they jumped into the pond and started to have their baths. One of the birds flew over to the crocodile and sat on the very end of its mouth.

A baby zebra saw this and asked its mother if the bird was going to be eaten.

"No, my dear," said the mother. "You see, that is not a real crocodile. We made it last night out of bits of wood. We made it to stop Hippopotamus getting in the pond."

"Will you tell him it's not a real one?" asked the baby zebra.

"Perhaps one day. When he's very smelly."

And both zebras jumped in and joined the other animals.

Hippopotamus Climbs a Tree

Hippopotamus was very hungry.

He was lying on the ground beneath a banana tree and his tummy was empty. He listened to it making rumbly noises - bloomp bloomp, bloomp bloomp. Then he listened to it making gurgly noises - gluggle luggle, gluggle luggle.

"All I want is one banana," Hippopotamus sighed. "But they are all at the top of the tree and I am at the very bottom."

He rolled over onto his back and looked at one of the biggest bananas on the tree. "Please fall off," he said to the banana.

But the banana just stayed where it was. It didn't want to fall off.

Hippopotamus got more and more hungry.

Just then a monkey ran past Hippopotamus and jumped up into the tree. He climbed until he reached the very top. Then he picked the biggest banana, opened it up and ate it all in one bite. He dropped the banana skin which landed on Hippopotamus' nose.

"Hey, that's not very nice!" said Hippopotamus. "I can't just eat a banana skin."

But the monkey only laughed at him and ran back home.

Hippopotamus stared at the tree and at the bananas growing at the very top. "How can I get a banana when they are so high up? I do wish I could climb like a monkey," he sighed.
Then he had an idea. After all, if monkeys could get up trees why shouldn't a hippopotamus too?

He looked carefully at the tree. It was smooth and there weren't any branches to hold onto. The tree was very thin and it swayed backwards and forwards as the wind blew. Hippopotamus thought that if he was very careful and climbed up the tree very slowly, he could get to the top. Then he could eat a banana.

Hippopotamus squeezed his front and back legs tightly around the tree and slowly started to climb. But then a strange thing began to happen. As he climbed up the tree, Hippopotamus saw that it was bending over. And the higher up the tree he climbed, the more it bent.

Even so, he still couldn't reach the bananas.

Higher and higher climbed Hippopotamus. And the higher he climbed up the tree the lower it bent down. Until the bananas were almost on the ground.

"Nearly there," said Hippopotamus as he got closer and closer to the top of the tree.

Soon he was so close to the bananas that he could smell them. His tummy gave an extra big rumble and he reached out to pick one.

But as he did one of the leaves on the tree started to tickle the end of Hippopotamus' nose. Of course, he couldn't let go of the tree to brush the leaf away because then he would fall off. So the leaf kept on tickling and tickling until Hippopotamus gave the most enormous sneeze.
"Atishoo!"

He sneezed again. "ATISHOO!"
And then again even more
loudly. "**ATISHOO!**"
Hippopotamus held on as
tightly as he could to the tree
but it was too smooth and
slippery.
He fell to the ground and
landed on his back.
THUD!

Now the tree no longer had a great big Hippopotamus on it. It started to unbend and stand up straight. Up it went faster and faster rising like a kite in a strong wind. At last it was pointing right back up into the sky.
And as soon as it did the bananas flew off the top of the tree.

But instead of falling down the bananas kept going up.
Up and up they went until they could get no higher.
Then they started to fall back to the ground. Slowly at first - then faster and faster.

Hippopotamus was still lying on his back when he saw the bananas going up into the air. Then he saw them coming back down again. He knew exactly where they were going to land - right on top of his head.

But then he had an idea.

As the bananas fell towards him Hippopotamus opened his mouth as wide as he could.

And one by one the bananas dropped straight into his mouth - plop, plop, plop!

Hippopotamus closed his mouth and ate all the bananas at once. There was a big smile all over his face.

The monkey who had climbed the tree before came back. He climbed up it again. But when he got back there were no bananas left at all.

"Where have they all gone?" cried the monkey. "I"m still hungry!"

Hippopotamus smiled some more and pointed to his fat, round tummy.

"They are all in there," he told the monkey. "You're not the only one who can climb trees you know. Hippos are the best banana trees climbers in the whole, wide world."